SNOWBOARD
SHAM

BY JAKE MADDOX

text by
Eric Stevens

STONE ARCH BOOKS
a capstone imprint

Jake Maddox JV books are published by
Stone Arch Books
a Capstone imprint
1710 Roe Crest Drive
North Mankato, Minnesota 56003

www.capstonepub.com

Library of Congress Cataloging-in-Publication Data
Names: Maddox, Jake, author. | Stevens, Eric, 1974- author. | Maddox, Jake.
  Jake Maddox JV.
Title: Snowboard sham / by Jake Maddox ; text by Eric Stevens.
Description: North Mankato, Minnesota : Stone Arch Books, [2019] | Series: Jake Maddox.
  Jake Maddox JV | Summary: When Will Pastora's family arrived at the Sorenson Resort
  for a family vacation he did not know that there was going to be a snowboarding
  competition. He enjoys snowboarding, but he is embarrassed to admit that he is only a
  beginner so he signs up at a higher level—and soon realizes that tackling the more difficult
  slopes is dangerous and that he needs some help to admit his error in front of his new,
  more experienced acquaintances.
Identifiers: LCCN 2019008761| ISBN 9781496584625 (hardcover) | ISBN 9781496584649
  (paperback.) | ISBN 9781496584663 (eBook PDF)
Subjects: LCSH: Snowboarding—Juvenile fiction. | Contests—Juvenile fiction. | Self-
  confidence—Juvenile fiction. | Embarrassment—Juvenile fiction. | Brothers and sisters—
  Juvenile fiction. | CYAC: Snowboarding—Fiction. | Self-confidence—Fiction. | Brothers
  and sisters—Fiction. | LCGFT: Sports fiction.
Classification: LCC PZ7.M25643 Snj 2019 | DDC 813.6 [Fic] —dc23
LC record available at https://lccn.loc.gov/2019008761

Designer: Dina Her

Photo Credits: Shutterstock: Brocreative, design element, BergeImLicht, (mountains) design
element, cluckva, (geometric) design element, Dmytro Vietrov, (snowboarder) cover

Printed in the United States of America.
PA70

TABLE OF CONTENTS

CHAPTER 1

THE COMPETITION

"There it is," Dad said.

It was Friday morning. Dad guided the family minivan carefully along the winding and snow-covered road, headed for their vacation destination.

In the seat at the far back, Will Pastora leaned forward to get a look. Ahead, a modest mountain, thick with pine trees, boasted a swath of cleared faces.

Ski slopes.

"Looks pretty good," Mom said.

"Not bad, I guess," Will said.

The truth was, since Dad took early retirement, the Pastora family had to cut back on a lot of expenses, including this winter's ski and snowboard trip. The last couple of years, they'd gone to a much nicer resort with bigger mountains and better snow.

This white stuff was probably man-made, icy and chunky. The resort was small, and there weren't many ski and snowboard trails. Hatchinson, the nearby town, was also small.

"Tilly says Hatchinson is super cute," said Will's big sister, Eve. Tilly was Eve's best friend. "Her family's been here a bunch of times."

Dad pulled the van into a sunken gravel parking area. The lodge loomed over the lot. The A-frame building cast a shadow and blocked out the bright sky.

A wooden sign hung across the building: *Sorenson Resort*. Beneath that a banner flapped in the icy winter breeze, reading: *Welcome Junior Snowboarders!*

"What do you think that means?" Will asked as he climbed out of the van.

Dad read the sign aloud. "They must mean you and Eve," he said.

"Right," Will said. "I'm sure they put up a banner just for the Pastora kids."

Dad crossed the lobby to get the family checked in at the main desk. Will, Eve, and Mom brought in the bags and gear. They set everything down at the porter's desk.

"I'd love to check out the town," Eve said. She sat down on her suitcase. "Tilly told me about a great coffee shop that also sells vintage clothes."

"Let's get settled in at the room first," Mom said. "I don't want to make Dad get right back in the van now that we're finally here."

"You can take the shuttle bus," said a boy walking by. He looked about Will's age. He had long, dark hair tied into a ponytail and wore a mismatched outfit of snowboarding pants, coat, and boots. "It leaves from right out front and goes directly into town. They go back and forth all day long."

The boy pointed out the front door. A small white bus was parked there, its engine running and its door open. Small black letters on the side of the bus said *SORENSON RESORT.*

"See?" he said. "It's there now."

"Is it free?" Eve asked.

The boy nodded. "I think so," he said. "I've never paid anything."

"Mom, can I?" Eve said, turning her pleading face toward Mom.

"I don't know," Mom said. "By yourself?"

"Mom!" Eve said. "I'm sixteen. I'll be fine."

Mom looked at her a moment and then over at Dad. He was still busy talking to the hotel clerk at the check-in desk.

Mom looked back at Eve. "Fine," she said. "But be sure to find out when and where the shuttle picks you up to come back, and don't stay too long."

"I won't," Eve said as she got up and ran for the bus.

"Do you have any money?" Mom called after her.

"Yes, Mom!" Eve said. She hopped on the bus. A moment later, the door closed and the shuttle sputtered away.

"Where's Eve going?" Dad asked as he walked over, keys in hand. He handed a card to the young woman at the porter's desk. She took it, smiled, and began moving the Pastoras' gear into the locked checkroom behind the desk.

"Into town," Mom said. "There's a shuttle."

"Alone?" Dad asked.

"She'll be fine," Mom said. She winked at Will.

"And who's this?" Dad asked. He smiled at the boy who had told them about the shuttle.

"I'm Jasper," the boy said.

Mom held Will by the shoulders. "This is Will," she said. "We'll be at the resort for the next few days."

"Hi," Will said.

"Well, I'm starved," Dad said, patting his stomach. "Who wants lunch?"

"I do," Mom said.

"Jasper," Dad said, "you're welcome to join us if your parents say it's okay."

"I already ate lunch," Jasper said.

"I'm not hungry either," Will said.

"Suit yourself," Dad said.

He handed Will a key with the number 302 engraved on its face. "Here's the key," he said, "but they're still cleaning the room. You won't be able to get in until three."

Will checked the clock hanging over the porter's desk. "That's almost two hours," he complained.

"I'll show you around," said the boy. "I've been here loads of times."

"You do seem to know your stuff," Mom said. "Sound okay to you, Will?"

Will shrugged. "I guess," he said. "Anything to do around here besides hit the slopes?"

"Not much," Jasper said. "But there's a TV in the lodge."

"Have fun, boys," Mom said. She and Dad walked off hand in hand toward the chalet's restaurant.

"This way," Jasper said. He led Will through the lobby toward a big open doorway. Beyond, Will could see the dark wood furniture of the lodge and the flickering orange glow of a fire.

"Are you here for the youth snowboarding competition too?" Jasper asked.

"Oh, that explains the banner," Will muttered to himself.

"What?" Jasper said.

"Nothing, nothing," Will said.

Of course, Will hadn't heard anything about the competition. But if this kid was in it, maybe it would be fine for Will to enter too.

"Yeah, I'm here for the competition," he said.

In a way, it was true. Now that he was here, he'd be in the competition. What difference did it make if he came up here just for that purpose? He didn't want to seem like he didn't know what was going on.

Besides, Will loved snowboarding. He'd gone two times before on his last two winter vacations.

"Did you sign in yet at the registration table?" Jasper asked as they stepped into the lodge.

There was a single step down into the lounge. Will stumbled a little. The room was darker than it had been in the lobby. It took a few moments for Will's eyes to adjust.

"Um, no," Will said. "Where is it?" He looked around the big, dark room, expecting to find a table where he'd sign in.

"It's not in here," Jasper said. "But we can cut through. Come on. It's over by the equipment rental shed. I'll show you the way."

CHAPTER 2

MORE LIES

Behind the main lodge, halfway down a paved path toward the rope tow for the bunny slope, sat a small metal building. A whole bunch of gear leaned against the wall.

"That's the rental and repair shop," Jasper said. "The check-in table is around back."

Jasper led Will around the back of the shop. There, a folding table had been set up bearing a banner: *JUNIOR SNOWBOARDING COMPETITION CHECK-IN.*

"Hey, Jasper!" called a boy who was leaning on the table. He was taller than Jasper and Will, and he wore a mischievous grin. His black hair—darker even than Will's—was buzzed super short. A nice-looking snowboard with one end in the snow leaned against his shoulder.

"Hey, Eli," Jasper said. "Finally checking in?"

"Not everyone feels the need to check in the instant they arrive at the resort, Jasper," Eli said. "Who's this guy?" He nodded at Will without looking at him.

"I'm Will," Will said.

"His family just checked in at the resort," Jasper said. "He's here for the race too."

"Actually, I—" Will started to say. He might have explained that his family was just here for a vacation, and that he didn't even know about the competition until a few minutes ago. But Eli cut him off.

"Well, step right up," Eli said, grabbing his board and moving to make room at the table for Will.

"Oh, thanks," Will said.

On the tabletop were a couple of clipboards, a bunch of pens, a stack of packets in binder clips, and some flyers about the competition. A young man in a ski-patrol parka sat there looking at his phone.

"Um, what do I have to do?" Will asked quietly so Eli and Jasper wouldn't hear.

"Last name?" the man said. He set aside his phone and pulled the stack of packets closer to himself.

"Pastora," Will said.

The man picked through the stack of packets. "With a *P*?" he asked.

"Yeah," Will said.

"You're not in here," the man said. "Did you register already?"

"I thought this was registration," Will said.

"This is check-in," the man said with a sigh. "You should have registered already."

"Oh," Will said.

He thought about having to explain to Jasper and Eli that he couldn't be in the competition because he wasn't registered. He'd have to admit he didn't know anything about it until he got to the resort.

"Here," the man said. He passed a clipboard to Will. "Fill this out."

Will picked up a pen and started filling out the form, hoping against hope that Jasper and Eli wouldn't notice what he was doing.

"Didn't you register already?" Jasper asked, looking over Will's shoulder. "I thought you said you came up for the competition."

"Oh, I did," Will said. He thought fast. "I guess my mom must have forgotten to register me."

"Ha," Eli said. "Does your mom pick out your clothes for you too?"

Will glanced up, but then chose to ignore him and finished filling out the form. The last question on the sheet asked Will to check off a skill level for the snowboard race: beginner, intermediate, or expert. He checked beginner, figuring that the higher two levels were mostly older kids, high schoolers probably.

"Beginner?" Eli said snidely.

"Huh?" Will said.

"I think my little sister is in the beginner race," Jasper said.

Will suddenly felt like a baby. He could tell his cheeks were getting red. In the cold mountain air, hopefully no one would notice.

"How old is she?" Eli said, sneering. "Like five?"

"She's eleven," Jasper said. "Nothing wrong with being a beginner."

"Oh, I'm not a beginner," Will said. "I've gone snowboarding plenty of times."

Two times, he thought, *but lots of runs each time. That makes plenty.*

"I just checked the wrong box," Will said. He laughed and added, "I meant to check intermediate."

He scribbled out the beginner box and put a dark *X* in the next box. "There," Will said. He handed the clipboard back to the man at the table.

The man gave him a long look, as if giving Will a chance to change back to beginner.

But Will said nothing. He'd race in the intermediate group. So what if he couldn't win? It would be better than racing on the bunny slope with a bunch of babies.

"Okay, Will," the man said, sighing again. "Registration is ten dollars."

"I don't have any money on me," Will said.

"Are you staying at the resort?" the man asked.

"Yes," Will said.

"We can charge the registration to your room," the man said.

"Okay," Will said. He'd explain it to his parents later. It was just ten bucks. They wouldn't mind.

"Are you done yet or what?" Eli said. "We want to get going."

The man handed Will a packet. "You're all set," he said.

"Thanks," Will said, taking the packet and opening the folder. There was a competition schedule—the first race would be Sunday morning—and a sheet of coupons to use in the chalet for free chicken wings and hot chocolate.

"Good," Eli said. "Now let's go for a run before it gets crowded after lunch."

"I'm in," Jasper said. "My board's locked up over there." He nodded toward the back of the lodge, where a whole bunch of skis, poles, and boards leaned against the lock-up rack.

"This trail looks pretty good," Eli said as he nodded toward a trail behind Will. "Not too crowded."

Will turned around and lifted his gaze. At the bottom of the trail—where riders boarded the lift to the middle and top of the slope—a sign said *Knight's Trail* next to a blue square, and *Emperor's Lightning* next to a black diamond.

The blue square, Will knew, meant intermediate skill was required to use that trail, while the black diamond meant expert skill was required.

Will was pretty sure even the blue run would be a challenge for him, nevermind the black diamond.

"What do you say, Will?" Jasper said. "Want to join us?"

"Yeah," Eli said. "Show us what we're up against in the race."

"On the black diamond?" Will said.

"Nah," Jasper said. "That one would kill me."

Eli laughed. "I could handle the black diamond," he said. "Jasper's too chicken."

"That's me," Jasper said. "Big chicken who is going leave you in my wake in the race on Sunday."

Will squinted as he looked up the mountain to where the lift dropped riders for the blue run. The first drop on that run didn't even look like a hill. It was so steep it looked like a bright white wall.

"I wish I could," Will said with a shrug. "But all

my gear is checked at the front desk. I can't get it till my parents come back from lunch."

"Aw, too bad," Jasper said.

"Will!" a woman called. "Will, honey! We're back from lunch!"

Will turned, and there were his mother and father stomping across the snow. They smiled from ear to ear, waving at him. They had no idea what showing up at that exact moment would mean for Will.

"Just in time," Eli said. He grinned. "Looks like you'll be able to board after all."

CHAPTER 3

WIPEOUT

Fifteen minutes later, Will sat between Jasper and Eli on the ski lift. He stared down at the slope that crisscrossed under the lift. His snowboard hung from one foot, the other unlatched for the ride and dismount at the top.

Jasper and Eli talked across him, but Will didn't listen. He could hardly hear them. He was too nervous about his first blue run.

It would be faster than he'd ever gone. There would be moguls. It would really test his skill with quick turns and good balance. He hoped his legs would be strong enough.

The ride alone—higher up a slope than he'd ever gone before—was already making his stomach do backflips.

Oh no, Will thought. *What if this run has backflips on it?*

He knew that was crazy—boarders only did flips and stuff on halfpipe runs and off huge jumps. And even then, no one *had* to do a backflip to finish a run. But his mind wasn't working very well.

The lift was close to the top. Ahead of them, the riders glided off their chair and slid gracefully away from the lift.

Will became even more nervous.

Their chair reached the exit point. Eli and Jasper stood. Their boards kissed the snow.

Will stood. He reached for something to hold on to as his board touched down, but his hand knocked into Eli's arm.

"Watch it!" Eli shouted, but it was too late.

Their boards crossed, and the boys slid away from the lift together, tangled up. They both fell to the snow at the bottom of the exit ramp. The few other boarders and skiers around laughed quietly.

"Are you guys all right?" Jasper said as he buckled his free foot into the board.

"*I'm* fine," Eli snapped as he stood up, giving Will a little shove as he did. "Your new friend has a few issues, though."

"Sorry," Will said. He stood up and planted his free foot firmly on the snow. "Um, I've only ever ridden two-seaters before. Getting off was kind of awkward."

Well, he thought, *that much is true, anyway.* He *had* only ridden two-seaters before.

"Just watch it from now on," Eli said. He pulled down his goggles and shuffled his board away to start his run. Within seconds, he was zooming off down Knight's Trail.

"Don't worry about Eli," Jasper said. "He talks big, but he's harmless."

"Got it," Will said.

"You all right?" Jasper asked as he pulled down his goggles. "I could wait if you want."

"I'm fine," Will said. He didn't need any babysitting on the slope. "Go ahead. I'll be right behind you."

Jasper smiled and hopped his board to the edge of the run. "See you at the bottom!" he called. Then he took off.

Will pushed with his free foot until he was just at the edge of the slope. He looked down. Eli and Jasper were already halfway down, where the blue probably turned into a green run. He could see the top of the tow rope from there.

That's where I should be, he thought. *I should have left my form as beginner. Then I wouldn't be stuck up here.*

Will sat down and strapped in his free foot. There would be no other way to handle this aside from riding the lift back down, but that would be the most embarrassing option.

"Might as well get it over with," he told himself.

He could go slowly. He knew how to turn. The worst that could happen was he would take a very long time getting down. He could handle that.

Will took a deep breath. He muttered to himself, "Here goes nothing."

With a little hop, he tipped the nose of his board over the edge of the slope and . . . *Zoom!*

In an instant, he was going too fast. He zipped past skiers and other snowboarders and shot straight down the hill as they all cut gracefully back and forth across the face.

"Sorry!" he shouted as he missed one skier by mere inches.

"Watch out!" he cried as he nearly collided with a snowboarder.

"Coming through!" he yelled as he zoomed right through a group of young skiers taking a lesson.

It had been only a few seconds since he left the top, and he'd already had three close calls. His luck would have to run out soon.

Ahead the trail curved to the left. Will leaned to try to force the board to turn, but nothing happened.

He pushed with his back foot to try to lean back a little and cut the back edge of his board into the snow, hoping to at least come to a stop and fall backward.

And fall he did, but not like he planned. At this speed, he couldn't make the board do what he wanted. When he pushed his back foot, the front edge of the board caught in the packed snow. Will tumbled forward, right into the tree line.

CHAPTER 4

BOARDING AT LAST

Will looked up at the sky. It was bluer now. A few wispy clouds streaked past.

"Ow," he said as he sat up.

He was a few feet into the trees, off the edge of the blue trail.

Will heard the sound of a snowboarder sliding up nearby and stopping.

"You okay?" a girl called to him.

He looked up. The girl stopped nearby and pulled up her goggles. She wore an orange helmet, a gold balaclava, and an orange and gold ski suit to match.

Unlike Will's outfit and the outfits most snowboarders wore, which were baggy pants and long, baggy parkas, her ski suit was fitted. It made her look a little like a superhero.

"Need some help?" the super girl asked. "Maybe blue trails are a little too much for you."

"I'm fine," Will said, embarrassed. "New boots are stiff. You know how it is."

The girl squinted at him a moment. She shrugged, replaced her goggles, and snowboarded off. Will watched her zoom away.

Will unstrapped his boots and picked up his board. With his board under one arm, and with his shoulder and ego bruised, he walked along the tree line until he reached the top of the tow rope and the start of the green run. He was glad his mom always made him wear a helmet. That fall would have been a lot worse without one.

He sat on the snow at the top of the green trail and put his board back on. Ahead was a wide, gentle slope. It was just the sort of trail Will was used to from his experience snowboarding in past winters.

Will hopped forward and slowly picked up speed. With ease, he pushed out with his heel and the board obeyed, swooping in a wide arc to the left.

Among the newbies and bunnies on the green trail, Will felt like an expert. While other riders struggled with their skis, boards, and poles, Will swooshed around them. He loved the sound of his snowboard on the icy machine-made snow.

He was smiling when he reached the bottom and came to a confident stop. He unstrapped one boot and lifted up his goggles to find Jasper and Eli standing nearby, waiting for him.

"Took you long enough," Eli said immediately. "I guess I don't have to worry about competition from you in the races on Sunday."

Shaking his head and laughing, Eli walked off, his board under his arm. "I'm going again," he said as he left. "Peace!"

"Hey, you wipeout up there?" Jasper asked.

"Me?" Will said, forcing a smile and laugh. "No way. Just had to stop to fix my boots a couple of times. They're new." They *were* new and a little stiff. That much was true.

"Uh-huh," Jasper said. He looked at Will's helmet.

"What?" Will asked.

"Nothing," Jasper said. "It's just that you have a huge scuff mark on your helmet like you crashed into something."

Will's hand instinctively went to his head. "Oh, no," he said quickly, still smiling his fake smile. "That was there already. Happened last season, I think."

"Oh," Jasper said. "I don't remember seeing it when you put your helmet on."

Will felt his face go red. He was glad the cold weather made it hard to tell he was blushing because of his lies.

"Wanna take another run?" Jasper asked. "Looks like Eli is still in line for the lift. We could catch up."

"Nah, you go ahead," Will said. "I'll find you guys later. I'm getting hungry. I'm gonna go find something to eat."

"All right," Jasper said. "See ya."

Will watched as Jasper pushed and glided his way to the chairlift again. He could tell Jasper and Eli were talking about him for a moment as he stood there. They both looked back at Will.

Finally, Will unstrapped his other boot, hefted his board under one arm, and headed for the lodge. He would have liked to take a few more rides up the tow rope and back down the green section. That part had been a lot of fun.

But he couldn't. Jasper and Eli would see, and they'd know he was really a beginner—and that he lied.

Will locked his gear outside and headed into the lodge.

"Will, over here!" Mom called, waving at him from a couch near the fireplace.

Will walked over and dropped onto the couch.

"We're about to hit the slopes," Dad said, "but there's something we have to talk to you about first."

"Uh-oh," Will said. "Sounds serious."

"The resort sends me a text to confirm every charge to the room," Dad said.

"Oh," Will said, remembering the competition fee. "I was going to tell you about that."

"Of course, it's fine with us if you want to race on Sunday," Mom explained. "In fact, we think it's great."

"But why not mention it to us first?" Dad asked.

"You were at lunch," Will said.

"But we saw you before you went riding with your two new friends," Mom pointed out. "You might have mentioned it then."

"I couldn't in front of—" Will started to say, but he stopped himself. He'd have to admit to lying to the two boys about being at the resort for the competition and not just a silly family vacation.

"Sorry," Will said. "I guess it slipped my mind. I was all excited about getting my gear and getting started on the slopes."

Dad smirked at him. Will could tell they weren't buying it.

"You were feeling embarrassed," Mom suggested, "that you'd have to clear spending ten dollars with your mom and dad, weren't you?"

That works, Will thought. "Yup," he said, relieved. "I was embarrassed. Sorry."

"Ah, we understand," Dad said. "We had parents once too."

"You still do," Will said.

"Let's not bring Grammy and Papa into this," Mom said. She stood up. "Ready, honey?"

Dad stood with a sigh. "Will we see you out there?" he asked Will.

"Sure," Will said. "I'll join you later."

As they left, though, he knew he'd told yet another lie. He wouldn't be out on the slopes again today.

CHAPTER 5

SECRET LESSONS

On Saturday morning, Will had breakfast at the lodge with his parents and sister. He made sure to get a seat facing the cafeteria line. The last thing he wanted to see was a pair of snowboarders named Jasper and Eli. But if he saw them first, maybe he could avoid them.

He couldn't handle another day trying to explain why he'd catch up, or why he couldn't take another run on the Knight's Trail, or, worse yet, try the Emperor's Lightning.

"Everything okay, Will?" Mom asked.

"Fine. Why?" Will asked. He realized he'd been fiddling with his paper napkin. Shreds of it sat in a messy pile next to his plate. Will shoveled some of his cheese omelet into his mouth to cover his anxiety.

"Oh, no reason," Mom said, grinning. "You just keep looking at the door, and then at the line, and then out the window, and then at the door."

"Mom's right," Eve said. She sipped her coffee. Eve had recently started drinking coffee with Mom and Dad every morning. The habit made Will roll his eyes.

"You look like the bad guy in a spy movie or something," Eve said. "Like someone whose worried there's a price on his head."

"Whatever," Will said.

"He's looking for his new friends," Dad said. He patted Will's leg. "Probably hoping to get out on his board with them before his mom and dad drag him out there."

"Oh, Will," Eve said. "That reminds me. I met a girl in town yesterday, and she's a snowboarding instructor here. She told me that if we're staying at the resort, lessons are included. So I signed up for one this morning."

"So?" Will said.

"*So* you could take one too," Eve said.

Will sat back in his chair and set a sideways glare on his sister. "Let me get this straight," he said. "You want *me*—your little brother who you wouldn't be caught dead with at the mall back home—to come with *you* to a snowboarding lesson with some girl you met in town."

Eve sighed. "Oh, whatever," she said. "I refused to go to the mall with you one time, like, two years ago. Anyway, after your wipeout yesterday, I thought you could use the help for the race tomorrow."

"Wipeout?" Mom said with concern.

"It was nothing," Will said.

"That's not what Melody said," Eve said.

"Who's Melody?" Dad asked.

He and Mom watched their children like the audience at a play. Mom thoughtfully chewed her blueberry muffin.

"She's the snowboarding instructor," Eve said.

"What would *she* know about it?" Will said.

"She saw it happen, dorkus," Eve said.

Will's mind flashed back to his crash and the girl who had seen him lying there among the trees—the girl who looked like a superhero.

"How did she know I was your brother?" Will asked as his heart fell into his stomach.

"We were chatting this morning," Eve said with a shrug, "and we put two and two together. She wanted me to make sure you weren't hurt."

"Will, honey," his mom said, leaning forward and putting a hand on his arm, "*are* you hurt?"

"I'm fine!" Will said. He pulled his arm away and scowled at his omelet. "Forget it. I'm not taking a lesson."

Even if he'd wanted to take a lesson—and he definitely didn't, especially not with the super girl as his teacher—he couldn't. What if Jasper and Eli saw? They'd know for sure he was lying about being as good as them.

"Well, I am," Eve said. She pushed back her chair and stood up. "And it starts soon."

"Have fun, sweetie," Dad said.

"See you on the slopes!" Mom said.

Dad sighed. "We ready to go?" he asked.

Will pushed away his now-cold cheese omelet.

"I am," Mom said.

"I'm not feeling great," Will said. Embarrassment and anxiety made him queasy. "I think I'll just sit here for a while longer. You two go ahead. I'll catch up later."

Dad and Mom exchanged a glance.

"Okay," Mom said. "Do you want a room key? You can go lie down."

"No," Will said. "I'll be fine in a minute."

"Come on," Dad said, taking Mom's arm. "He just wants to be on his own when his friends show up. So he looks cool."

"He always looks cool!" Mom said.

"Please," Will said, "go away."

"Fine, fine," Dad said. Will's parents left.

He watched them go. Suddenly he had a plan. His queasiness faded as he waited a few moments. Then he hurried to grab his gear at the lock-ups outside.

From the bottom of the nearest green run, he could see the class gathering at the top of the tow rope. He spotted his sister's green and pink helmet.

He spotted the superhero girl in her fitted orange and gold uniform. There were only five or six students. They all seemed between his age and Eve's.

Quickly, Will strapped in one boot and pushed himself to the bottom of the tow ropes. It was still early, and the line was short. Before long, he was gripping the rope tightly and being pulled up the side of the slope.

The class started down the slope. He watched from the top as Melody led her students in a slow descent.

Will strapped in his second foot and hopped to the edge. He followed the same line the class had, keeping an eye on Melody and straining to hear her as he went.

He kept his back edge in the snow and glided across the hill. Before he reached the tree line, he twisted his body, pushing the back of his board behind him and pushing down with his left heel.

The board swiveled easily at this speed. Will cut back the other way, toward the opposite edge of the hill. "This is too easy," he said to himself, feeling pleased. Compared with yesterday's disaster, this felt great.

Below, the class had stopped. They huddled together at the top of the bunny slope—the widest part at the very bottom of the green trail—where a group of young kids were taking a ski lesson without poles.

"I want to try some stops now," Melody said to the class.

Will stopped on the other side of the top of the bunny slope. He tried to act naturally as he listened in on the lesson.

"Everyone," Melody went on, "I want you to stay along this side of the slope. Watch out for the little ones. As you reach the bottom, cut hard and come to a stop. Be sure not to let your front edge catch. That will put you on your face. If you sit back to stop, that's fine. Land on your rear."

She pulled on her goggles. "Follow me and do what I do," she said.

She pushed off. Along the right side of the hill, Melody built up a lot of speed. She made a dozen little turns back and forth to control her speed, but she never strayed from the right side of the hill.

The tail end of her board swished back and forth as she leaned backward and quickly shifted her right foot. Each swish was like a very quick turn. It was a good way to maintain speed without going too fast and losing control.

At the bottom, she cut her right foot hard, making a much sharper turn and lifting the toe edge of her board. She stopped, reached down, popped out her right boot, and turned around.

"Come on, guys!" she called up the slope. "Show me what you can do!"

Eve went first. She had a harder time flicking her back foot side to side, so she ended up going a little too fast. But at the bottom, she managed to bring her right foot around and lift her downward edge. The board stopped, and she sat back, dropping her rear to the snow.

Will watched the rest of the class do the same thing. One person went way too fast and zipped right past Melody at the bottom. He finally managed to stop by grabbing hold of the trail map sign.

When the class was all done and lined up for the chairlift to the next part of the lesson, Will went down.

Staying left, he tried to avoid being spotted by Eve and the others in the class. His back foot obeyed him at first, letting him cut in a quick line as he zipped down. The tree line on his left was a blur as he picked up speed.

Too much speed.

Soon his back foot stopped doing what he wanted. He struggled to slow down and ended up too far to the right.

"Sorry!" he called out as he zipped too close to a group of older skiers.

He felt himself making the same mistakes his sister made. Before he'd quite reached the bottom, he pushed his back foot hard to the right, trying to lift the front edge of his board as he swiveled.

But his speed got the better of him. His board cut fast to the left and into a tight circle. Next thing he knew, Will fell forward and got a face full of snow.

He pushed himself up and got onto his knees. His goggles were fogged up and packed with icy snow, so he pulled them off as he spit bits of grit from his mouth.

"You okay?" a familiar voice asked.

"I'm fine," Will said. He looked up. "Oh, it's you."

Eve smiled down at him. "You could have just joined the lesson," she said, "instead of trying to sneak around."

"Did everyone see?" Will asked.

Eve took a moment to answer.

"I'll take that as a yes," Will said.

"Sorry," Eve said. "I'm sure Melody wouldn't mind if you joined now."

Will shook his head. "I think I'll just go back to the lodge for a little while," he said.

"I need to get back to the group," Eve said.

Will nodded.

Eve pushed off to rejoin the class. Will watched as she lined up for the lift with Melody at the back of the group. Both girls looked over at him for a moment just as Jasper and Eli had yesterday.

I wonder if saying you don't want a lesson, Will thought, *and then sneaking around to take a lesson anyway counts as lying.*

Then he thought, *I'm the laughing stock of Sorenson Resort. At least if I just sit in the lodge and drink cocoa, it can't get any worse.*

CHAPTER 6

SQUIRE'S FALL

Will slouched down on the comfy little couch close to the fireplace at the lodge and watched the big TV behind the bar.

His empty cocoa cup sat next to him on a small table. He'd finished it two hours ago, but he was too down to throw out the cup or get a refill from the coffee stand.

Besides, there was always a little crowd gathered at the coffee stand. They'd probably recognize him as Will Pastora, newbie snowboarder and infamous liar.

"This seat taken?" asked a familiar voice.

"It's a free country," Will said.

His sister dropped into the seat next to him and handed him a paper cup. "Mint cocoa?" she offered.

Will glanced at her an instant. "Thanks," he said, taking the cup. It smelled great. He loved mint in his cocoa, but he hadn't been sure the coffee stand had any mint syrup.

"Why aren't you out there tearing up the slopes?" Eve asked. "You're not going to let a couple of crashes ruin your vacation, are you?"

"Maybe," Will said.

"Come on," Eve said. "Last winter, you and I both wiped out on our boards a dozen times each! That didn't stop us from having a good time."

"This winter it's stopping me," Will said.

"That's not like you," Eve said. "You're a lot of things, Will, but you're not a quitter."

"Says who?" Will said. "I can be a quitter if I want to."

Eve shook her head. "Nope," she said. "You can't quit. For two reasons. One: I will not have my last name ruined forever by my annoying little brother."

"Ha-ha," Will fake laughed.

"And two," Eve went on, "you already spent ten dollars to register for that race. You have to compete, or Mom and Dad will *not* be happy."

Will hadn't thought of that. "I'll pay them back," he said. "I have ten dollars in my save jar at home."

He sighed. "Look, it's worse than you think," he finally admitted. "I let Jasper and Eli—the two guys I met—think that I was as good as they are. When I registered, I signed up as intermediate instead of a beginner. That means I'll have to race on really tough trails—too tough for me."

Eve's eyes widened and she nodded. "For me too, I bet," she said. "Why'd you do that?"

Will shrugged. "I don't know," he said. "I guess I didn't want them thinking I was a baby."

"Will," Eve said. "I'm sixteen. *I* am not a baby, but I also can't really take on the blue runs yet. I know I'm getting better, though, and someday I'll be able to."

"It's different for you," Will said. "You're a girl. Your friends won't make fun of you if you're not as good at a sport as they think you should be."

"First of all, ha," Eve said. "That's a laugh. Girls don't make fun of each other? You obviously haven't met enough girls. And besides, who says Jasper or Eli will make fun of you?"

"Eli already has," Will said. "Every chance he gets. He definitely wouldn't leave me alone if I raced in the beginner category."

"What about Jasper?" Eve asked.

"He's actually pretty nice. I don't think he'd make fun of me," Will admitted. "But it's even worse with him. His little sister is in the beginner race! She's eleven!"

"You were eleven too," Eve said, "like eighteen months ago. That's not a very big difference. And if their family goes to ski resorts a lot, then of course they're better snowboarders. So what?"

Will didn't know what to say. Eve was only a few years older, but she'd obviously already forgotten what middle school kids were like.

"I have a solution for you," Eve said, "and it won't cost you a penny. Melody the instructor is basically my new best friend, and she would be happy to give you a free private lesson this afternoon when she gets off work."

Will nearly gasped with horror. "Um, I don't think so," he said. "I'd be way too embarrassed."

"I'd be there too," Eve said. "I promise she won't laugh at you."

"There's no way you can know for sure she won't laugh at me," Will said.

"Okay, then if she does," Eve said, "I'll dump her as my new best friend forever and you and I will leave her on the side of the hill and never look back."

Will actually laughed. "Fine," he said. "One lesson. But if this is some kind prank you two are playing on me . . ."

Eve raised one hand and said, "No prank. All good intentions. I swear."

* * *

That afternoon Will and Eve met Melody at the top of the trail called Squire's Fall.

"A squire, like a knight's student?" Will asked.

Melody nodded. She wasn't in her resort uniform anymore, so she didn't look like a superhero—just a regular girl.

"And 'fall,'" Will said. "What do you think that means?"

"Probably dying in battle or something," Eve said.

"So this trail is named for a student dying," Will said, looking down the gentle slope toward the lodge. "Great."

Melody smiled at him. "I promise," she said, "no one has died on Squire's Fall."

"No instructions this time," she went on. "We'll just go down together, nice and easy, and I'll give you tips at the bottom. Think you can handle that?"

"Yes," Will said.

"And you won't try anything crazy," Melody said, "like snowboarding off the trail and into the trees, right?"

Will sighed. "Right," he said.

"Ready?" Melody asked, glancing at Eve.

Eve nodded. The three boarders buckled in, pulled down their goggles, and slid off the edge.

Will's shoulder was stiff from yesterday's wipeout, and his legs weren't in great shape, either. But on the beginner slope—and with some emotional support from Eve—Will kept his turns smooth.

He loved the sound of his board's base whispering over the fresh-laid snow. His spirit soared as his legs and feet worked with him, pulling the tail to turn right, urging it forward to raise the toe edge to turn left.

He cut across the wide trail over and over, keeping up with Melody and Eve. He was sure Melody wasn't exactly trying her hardest, but it felt good to stick with the older riders without much trouble.

At the bottom, Will twisted to a perfect stop alongside his sister and teacher.

"Nice!" Melody said, putting out her palm. "I didn't even see anything to work on."

Will pulled up his goggles and rolled his eyes.

"Come on, Will. Don't leave me hanging." Melody waved her hand.

Will laughed and slapped her hand. "All right," she said. "Let's go again."

They spent the afternoon going up and down Squire's Fall. With each run, Will's legs got stronger, and his spirit grew more confident. By the time the sun began to dip behind the mountain, the three riders were laughing and having fun.

"It's almost dark," Melody said when all three gathered at the bottom after their fastest run so far, "and I have to be home for dinner. But let's take one more run."

"Sure," Will said. He headed for the lift to the top of Squire's Fall.

"Uh-uh," Melody said, grabbing his arm. She nodded behind her. "Let's try Knight's Trail one time."

Will looked at Eve, who nodded eagerly. "I'm game," she said.

"I don't know," Will said. "You saw what happened to me last time."

"That was before a half day of lessons with the best teacher on the mountain," Melody said.

"Come on, bro," Eve said. "You did it for those two kids you met yesterday. Do it for me."

"All right," Will said. He looked toward the top of Knight's Trail and his heart tumbled in his chest. "Let's go."

CHAPTER 7

KNIGHT'S TRAIL

Will made sure to avoid the middle seat on the chairlift this time.

It was almost night on the mountain. The lights clicked on, casting a golden glow over the slopes. It made the woods at the edges of the trails look even darker and scarier.

The icy wind across the mountain became cold and hard, especially up on the lift. Their chair swung in the wind. Will held tight to the bar in front of them.

"You got this, bro," Eve said.

"For sure," Melody said, leaning forward a little. "You're a super quick learner, and you definitely have some natural talent for snowboarding."

"Really?" Will said, shocked. "Then why do I fall so much?"

"I didn't see one wipeout this afternoon," Melody said.

That was true, Will knew. Still—he wasn't feeling very confident.

Melody lifted the bar. They were almost to the exit ramp.

"Ready?" she said. "I'll go left, Eve, go straight, and Will, you go to the right. Don't start down without me."

I can do this, he thought. He kept his eyes on the ramp. He was careful to stand without pushing off his sister or the chair, but to just let the ramp and his board guide him down and to the right.

He took a deep breath, stood up, and placed his right boot on the back of his board. His left boot was already strapped in.

With ease, he slid to the right, leaning a little over the toe edge as he went. In a moment, Melody and Eve joined him at the top of Knight's Trail.

"Nicely done," Melody said. "Will, I want you to go down first. Eve and I will follow behind you."

"Me?" Will said. "You want me to lead?"

"Sure," Melody said, pulling down her goggles. She bent over to strap in her right foot. "That way I'll be able to watch your technique as you go. This lesson is mostly for you, right?"

"Makes sense, I guess," Will said.

"Whenever you're ready, then," Melody said.

Will pulled on his goggles. Eve did the same.

"Here goes nothing," Will said. He hopped over the edge.

In the golden light of the night lamps, the first drop felt otherworldly. Everything Melody had taught him that day seemed almost second nature.

He picked up speed quickly, but he knew he could hold the turns. He cut back and forth across the face of the trail, just as Melody had taught him. It was just like the green run, but faster.

He smiled as the icy night wind cut into his cheeks. He shortened up his turns, allowing him to move a little faster and to keep his board's nose pointing more steeply downhill.

Will loved the feel of picking up speed, and he loved the sound of the icy machine-made snow as his tail swished back and forth.

"Slow down, Will!" Melody called behind him.

"I'm fine!" he shouted back, though he was sure the wind carried his voice away and Melody didn't hear.

Ahead, after a steeper drop, the trail cut to the left. Will recognized the spot as where he'd crashed the day before.

"Not this time," he said to himself. He gritted his teeth and turned hard to the left to take the steep section at a diagonal.

As he reached the bottom of the steep section,

though, he was going too hard into the left turn. Before he could slow down, he overturned.

For an instant, his nose was pointing back uphill before the toe edge caught the packed snow of the trail and sent him face-first into a wipeout. If not for the board acting like a brake behind him, he would have slid all the way into the woods again.

A few seconds later, Melody and Eve slid to a stop beside him.

"So much for natural talent," Will said. He rolled over onto his back and pulled up his knees.

"Don't be ridiculous," Melody said. She put out her hands to pull him up. "Everyone wipes out sometimes."

Will grabbed her hands and let her pull him up.

"You okay to finish the run?" Eve asked.

"Yeah, I'm fine," Will said. "A little embarrassed."

"Pff," Melody said. "You're out here after dark, working hard. Nothing embarrassing about that."

"I guess," Will said.

"Besides," Eve said, "from what I've seen on this run, if you're just a little more careful on that last turn, you'll be fine in that intermediate race tomorrow."

"Race?" Melody said. "You're in the competition tomorrow?"

Will nodded.

"In *intermediate*?" Melody asked.

Will looked away.

"I guess I shouldn't have said anything," Eve said. "But yeah, he is."

"Look, Will," Melody said. "You're a fast learner and you're doing well. But I don't think riding in the intermediate group is a good idea. It's not just Knight's Trail—it's the snowboard cross trail, a lot of competitors all in there together. Jumps, hard turns, drops—it'll be a rough ride."

"Too late now," Will said. "I registered intermediate."

Melody pulled her goggles back on. "Not necessarily," she said.

"What do you mean?" Will asked.

"Let's finish this run," Melody said. "I have some people to talk to in the lodge before I head home for the day."

With that, she took off down the mountain. By the time Will and Eve finished their run down the green portion, Melody was long gone.

CHAPTER 8

FESSING UP

"I don't think I can do this," Will said. He and Eve walked toward the check-in table on Sunday morning.

"You'll be fine," Eve said. "Melody handled it."

"I know," Will said. He turned around and found Eli and Jasper heading their way. "That's not the part I'm worried about."

"Hey, you two," Melody said as they stepped up to the table. She was back in her superhero resort uniform.

She looked at Will. "Ready to race?" she asked.

"I think so," Will said.

Eli and Jasper stepped up next to him.

"There he is," Eli said. "What happened to you yesterday?"

"Yeah," Jasper said. "We didn't see you all day."

"Oh," Will said. His voice shook with nervousness. "I was around."

Eli looked over the paperwork on the table. "Isn't this the beginner race check-in table?" he asked.

"Must be," Jasper said. "The intermediate races are later this morning."

"So what are you doing signing in here?" Eli asked.

"I know you made a mistake on the form," Jasper said, "but I thought you fixed that mistake."

Will glanced at Eve. She nodded at him.

"My mistake was changing my skill level back when I signed up," Will said.

"What do you mean?" Jasper asked.

Melody smiled at him.

Will turned and faced Jasper and Eli. "I should have left it as beginner," he said. "My mistake was lying and saying I was an intermediate snowboarder."

Jasper stared at him, but Eli laughed. "I bet Jasper's little sister will beat you in the race too," he said. "What a newb."

With that, Eli walked away, still laughing.

"Sorry," Will said to Jasper. "For lying, I mean."

"You should have just said you were a beginner," Jasper said. "Who cares? I would have gone with you on the greens or helped you out on the blues. Then I wouldn't have had to spend my entire day with him." Jasper thumbed over his shoulder toward Eli.

Will laughed. "Good point," he said.

"Good luck in the race," Jasper said, "but of course I'll be rooting for my sister."

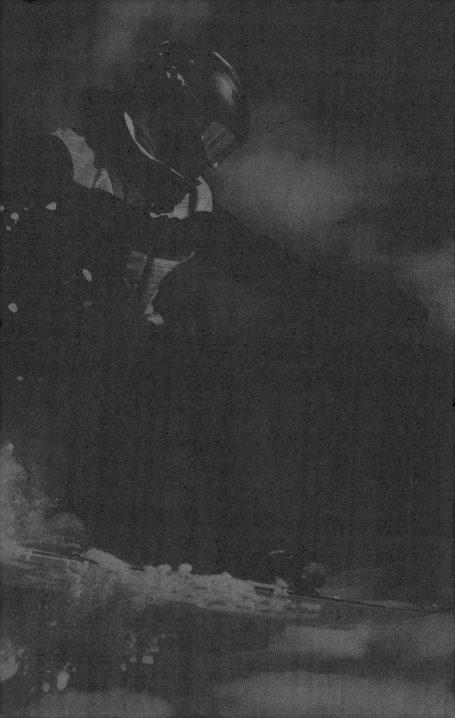

CHAPTER 9

TIME TO RACE

The first round of the beginner competition was a downhill race with staggered starts on a green circle called Apprentice's Wand. It was a new trail for Will. The day before, the crew had been preparing it for the competition, so no one could practice on it.

Every thirty seconds, a pair of racers started together. That way the slope wouldn't get too crowded.

Though they were all beginners, some displayed more skills than others.

The top four riders would move on to the final race.

Will and his starting partner were the first racers to start. Will lined up at the start and strapped on his board. A few feet away at the other gate was his starting partner, a girl who looked a little younger than him.

"I'm Essa," she said.

"Will," he replied. "Are you Jasper's sister?"

"Oh, yeah," she said. "He told me you'd be in the race too. My biggest competition." She pulled down her goggles.

"Okay, you two are our oldest beginner boarders," said the judge at the top of the slope. He was the same young man who had gotten Will registered on Friday. "So you're going first and hopefully fastest. We don't want to clog up the trail."

"That's kind of depressing, isn't it?" Essa said to Will out of the side of her mouth. "I guess we'll be racing against a bunch of babies."

"I only go snowboarding once a year," Will said. "I guess I'm doing all right. And you'll probably be racing black diamonds before you're out of middle school."

"So true," Essa said with a smile.

"Riders ready?" the judge asked.

Will wished Melody was the starting judge. He laughed to himself. This time yesterday she was an intimidating superhero. Now she was his friend.

"Ready," Essa said. She gripped the sides of the starting gate with both hands and slid her board forward and back, ready to push off.

"Ready," Will said, copying Essa. He figured she'd raced before and probably knew what she was doing.

"Set," the judge said. He blew his whistle, and they pushed off.

Essa took off to an early lead, swooshing her tail back and forth, knocking up fresh powder behind her. She let out a loud "Woohoo!" as she sped down the slope.

Will followed behind, taking the unfamiliar trail a little more carefully. Remembering his last crash yesterday, he kept his turns wide and his speed down.

As he reached what looked to be about the halfway mark, he heard the whistle behind him. That meant it had been thirty seconds. He was on track for finishing the run in a minute.

Ahead, Essa had a pretty good lead on him. He wondered if a minute for the whole run was a good time and if he had a chance of doing well.

Essa took a sharp curve and rode out of sight.

Will reached the turn. It reminded him of the blue run yesterday after dark. He bent his knees slightly and pushed out his tail with the heel of his right foot. Snow flared up in front of him in an icy poof.

The trail slid into a narrow, almost flat stretch through the woods. He could see Essa ahead as she left the narrow section.

Will slid easily here, smoothly along the packed trail. He used his back foot to move the tail of his board back and forth like a fish's tail. It felt good, and it felt easy.

Coming out of the woods, the trail took a right turn down a short, steep drop. Will reacted without thinking, switching his back foot, raising his heel side, and taking the turn in a tight, smooth arc.

The trail opened wide again, and now Will could see the lodge at the bottom. He saw his parents and sister standing near the finish line.

Mom waved up at him. Will raised one hand as he cut across the last descent.

He took the last fifty yards as fast as he could. Ahead, Essa crossed the finish.

Will crouched as he rode and let gravity take him as fast as it would. He zoomed across the finish and kicked his back foot forward, raising the toe edge and sending a spray of powder over the front row of spectators. He slid to a stop next to Essa.

People clapped. Eve hooted and cheered.

"Nice finish," Essa said. "But I beat you."

"You sure did," Will said. "Nice going."

"Thanks," Essa said.

"Clear out, you two," Melody called to them from the nearby judge's table. "The next pair will be finishing soon."

The pair of racers headed to the judge's table.

"Want your times?" Melody asked. "Will, fifty-seven seconds. Essa, fifty-two seconds."

"Is fifty-seven good?" Will asked.

"Not as good as fifty-two," Essa said.

"It's very good," Melody said. "I think you both have a good chance of moving on to the final round."

CHAPTER 10

JUMPS, DROPS, AND CURVES

Will *did* qualify for the final round. He, Essa, and a pair of ten-year-old riders would race in the final that afternoon.

After they got the results, Will and Essa went to join the spectators at the bottom of Magician's Goblet, a blue square trail on the east side of the mountain. The trail was taped off to be a bit narrower than normal. Blue lines had been painted at the peaks of several small jumps so the riders would see the drops as they approached.

Jasper and Eli would be racing that course.

"There they are!" Essa said. She pointed and waved enthusiastically toward the top of the slope.

Will squinted to see the top, shielding his eyes with one gloved hand. He saw two riders at the starting gate.

"How can you tell?" Will said.

"Trust me," Essa said. "I can tell."

The whistle blew, and the pair of riders pushed off. Both seemed to leave the ground for an instant as they came over the first drop and nose-dived down the slope.

Each kept his speed up, riding hard into the first curve. It was a wide right, and the riders seemed to hold on by a thread as their toe edges cut like knives into the packed snow.

The racers were neck and neck as they disappeared into a section hidden by woods.

"That's the best part," Essa said. "Remember the woods part on Apprentice?"

Will nodded.

"Well, on this trail," Essa said, "it's even better. Jumps, drops, sharp curves. It's super fun."

"You've done this trail?" Will asked, impressed. "I thought you were a beginner."

"I am," Essa said. "I didn't say it was easy. But it will be someday. For you too."

Will smiled. He turned his eyes back to the race just as the two riders appeared out of the woods. One rider had a small lead now—it looked like Jasper.

"Go, Jassy, go!" Essa shouted, jumping up and down and waving her arms. "Woo!"

Jasper crouched at the top of the last descent. Eli was right behind him. Halfway down the last drop, they reached a series of small jumps. They both got air.

Jasper came out of the jumps first. He crouched even lower and zoomed across the finish line just a second before Eli.

Jasper skidded to a stop right in front of Essa and Will.

"Nice going, Jassy!" Essa said. She threw her arms around her brother.

"Please don't call me *Jassy*," he said as he pulled off his goggles. "It sounds like *gassy*. I've told you a million times."

Eli swooshed up next to him. "I'll get you next time," he said.

"No doubt," Jasper said. They high-fived.

Before long, the intermediate qualifier was over. Jasper and Eli came in first and second place. They'd both be in the final round.

"Top four riders from each division," the finishing judge announced through her megaphone, "head over to Knight's Trail. The races will begin in fifteen minutes, starting with the intermediate final."

* * *

In the final intermediate race, all four riders started together.

"Remember," Essa said to Will as they watched from the bottom of the Knight's Trail, "Jasper is wearing the green helmet, and Eli is wearing the black one."

The other two riders were both high school age, one girl and one boy.

The whistle blew, and all four riders launched off the edge together.

Eli took an early lead after the first drop. He led the racers into the first curve, a wide right under the chairlift. Jasper stayed close to Eli. The bigger kids took the sharp curve neck and neck. As the riders reached the narrow section, the high schoolers took over the lead.

Jasper cut across the face of the hill and rode with the tree line close to his heel edge. At the entrance to the wooded trail, he took the sharp turn and the lead.

The high school kids took the turn a bit wider and kept Eli at the back of the pack.

"They'll come out over there," Essa said, pointing to a spot on the lower section, where it became Squire's Fall. Will remembered that trail well.

A moment later, Jasper shot out of the woods. One of the high schoolers was right behind him. The other came out a few seconds later, neck and neck with Eli.

On the last drop, Jasper almost wiped out on a patch of bad snow. His shoulder scraped the snow. He dragged one hand and pushed up to get back up on his board, sending up a spray of icy powder. He lost a little speed, and the high schooler passed him.

Trailing, Eli crouched and took the descent at superspeed, barely passing the other high schooler in the last few instants.

As the four riders swooshed into the finish area, the crowd cheered. The high schooler who had overtaken Jasper came in first.

"Jasper got second!" Essa said.

He and Eli popped off their back boots and pushed over to Will and Essa.

"Nice race, guys," Will said.

"Not for us," Eli said. "We didn't win."

Jasper shrugged. "I did pretty well," he said. "Might have won if not for that icy patch at the end."

"For sure," Essa said.

"You two better get ready for your race," Jasper said. "One of you might be the new beginner champion at Sorenson Resort."

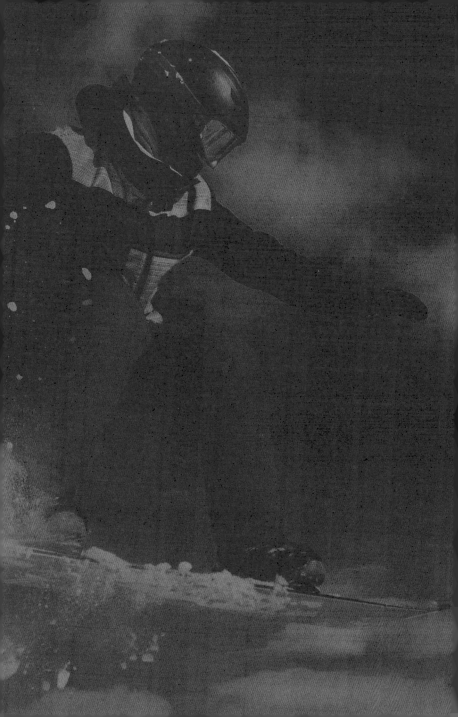

CHAPTER 11

FINAL ROUND

The beginners' final round was on Squire's Fall after lunch. The crew had spent the morning getting it ready for the race.

The resort had bananas and sandwiches for the racers. "I can't eat," Will said.

Essa nodded. "Me either," she said. "Too excited."

"And nervous," Will said.

"Maybe a little," Essa admitted.

Just like the intermediate race, all four qualifiers started together.

Essa and Will rode the chairlift together.

"Nervous?" Will asked.

"Nah," Essa said. "I've done this run a million times."

"Me too," Will said. "I probably went up and down this hill thirty times yesterday afternoon with Melody, the instructor."

"Oh, I know her!" Essa said. "I did a class with her last month. She took me down Magician's Goblet and showed me to the woods trail."

Essa laughed. "I wiped out so many times in there," she said. "She really helped me a lot."

"Me too," Will said.

At the top, the two riders glided off the lift and joined the other two qualifiers at the starting gates.

"Good luck," Essa said.

"You too," Will said.

They each took their spots at the starting gates.

Will looked up and down the starting line. There was Essa beside him. The two younger riders were on her other side, one in a green helmet and one in purple. They slid back and forth inside their gates, ready to start. The sound of the four boards on the packed snow almost sounded like breathing.

"Riders ready?" the starting judge said.

Will was ready.

"Set," the judge said.

He blew his whistle, and all four riders pushed off.

Will took a quick lead. Essa rode very close behind on his left. The two others were slower to start, but they gained speed easily.

Coming into the first left-hand curve, both younger riders passed him and Essa. Neither of them seemed to worry about slowing down at all. They just zoomed along the trail, taking the turn at top speed, while Will and Essa both slowed down a little.

The trail straightened at a drop and then cut hard to the right and under the chairlift. Here Essa cut loose. She crouched into the curve, cutting hard on her toe edge, and passed both younger riders.

Will followed at the rear. He lifted his heel edge, but he couldn't hold the speed as well as the others. At the next drop, he leaned hard and crouched, hoping to gain some speed. It was enough to catch the rider in green.

Ahead, Essa and the purple boarder fought for first place.

As they came around the last curve and out of the wooded area, Will saw the lodge and the finish line below.

The gathered crowd cheered as the racers entered the last stretch. Will took the steep drop as aggressively as he could. He held onto his lead over the younger rider in green.

Ahead, he watched Essa and the other young rider, both crouched as they came off the last steep drop and zoomed along the flat section across the finish line. Essa won.

Will crossed the finish line alone, and the rider in green finished close behind.

"Great race!" Essa said, giving him a high five as he skidded to a stop beside her. Nearby were Jasper, Melody, and Will's family.

They all cheered for him and Essa.

"Third place," Eve said, hugging him. "You'll get a bronze medal!"

"Great job," Jasper said. "My first time in the competition, I didn't even qualify for the final round."

"And look at him now," Essa said.

Will laughed and said, "Shows what a little practice will do."

ABOUT the AUTHOR

Eric Stevens lives in St. Paul, Minnesota. He is studying to become a middle school English teacher. Some of his favorite things include pizza, playing video games, watching cooking shows on TV, riding his bike, and trying new restaurants. Some of his least favorite things include olives and shoveling snow.

GLOSSARY

balaclava (bal-uh-KLAH-vuh)—a close-fitting cap that covers the head, neck, and tops of shoulders

chalet (sha-LAY)—a building with a roof that sticks far out past the walls; at a ski resort, chalets often house restaurants and lounge areas

infamous (IN-fah-muhss)—having a bad reputation

intentions (in-TEN-shuhns)—things you mean to do

intimidating (in-TIM-uh-date-ing)—frightening

mischievous (MISS-chuh-vuhss)—showing a spirited, playful behavior that may cause annoyance or harm to others

modest (MOD-ist)—not large or extreme

moguls (MO-guhls)—mounds of hard snow on a ski slope

porter (POR-tur)—someone who carries luggage for people at a hotel or resort

qualifier (KWAHL-uh-fye-ur)—a race that determines who will go on to the next level of a competition; also racers who advance to the next level

vintage (VIN-tij)—refers to items made in the past, or having the characteristics of old-fashioned items

DISCUSSION QUESTIONS

1. By lying to Jasper from the start, Will started a whole chain of lies. In your own words, explain how one lie led to another.

2. Explain how Jasper reacts when he learns that Will had lied. Put yourself in his place. Would you have a similar reaction or not?

3. Discuss how Will's lies almost ruined his vacation.

WRITING PROMPTS

1. Imagine Will never confessed to his lies and tried to race in the intermediate level. Write a race scene. What happens? How does he do? Does he get hurt?

2. Will tells his sister: "You're a girl. Your friends won't make fun of you if you're not as good at a sport as they think you should be." How do you feel about this statement? Write a paragraph or two about your reaction.

3. Will felt embarrassed when he had difficulty getting off the chairlift. Write about a time you were embarrassed. What happened and how do you feel now looking back at the memory?

MORE ABOUT
SNOWBOARD CROSS

Snowboard cross, also known as boardercross, is a snowboard racing sport. Though not as well known as halfpipe—the one with all the cool tricks—snowboard cross has been an event in the Winter Olympics since 2006.

Unlike the halfpipe event, which is scored by judges based on tricks, snowboard cross is a race against other boarders. The race takes place on a short trail, much like skiing, but with steep drops, jumps, and curves built into the trail. The curves are banked—just like the curves in a stock car race.

The riders in a snowboard cross race often wear protection, from a mouth guard to body armor. At high speeds and on narrow courses, it's essential to keep riders safe in the event of a collision.

Unlike many riders in halfpipe competitions, who are known for their baggy snowboarding fashion, boardercross racers wear fitted clothes to prevent getting snagged on other riders or even the poles that mark edges of the course itself.

Here's a look at the Olympic gold-medal winners since the sport's first appearance in the games in 2006:

Games	Men	Women
2006 Turin	Seth Wescott United States	Tanja Frieden Switzerland
2010 Vancouver	Seth Wescott United States	Maëlle Ricker Canada
2014 Sochi	Pierre Vaulitier France	Eva Samková Czech Republic
2018 Pyeongchang	Pierre Vaultier France	Michela Moioli Italy